Life's Touch
All Walks of Life

By

CLINTON X

AUTHOR'S NOTE

These short stories are works of fiction. All the characters, organizations, and events portrayed in the stories are either products of the author's imagination or are used fictitiously.

CONTENT

A COLLECTION OF SHORT STORIES

BOOK INRODUCTION

This book is a collection of short stories, an assortment of human experiences and interactions that seek to express how the simplest parts of our humanity are often the most complex and vice versa. This is a book of stories about the joy, pain, love, loss, indifference, silence, and awkward realities that make up the human predicament. As you journey through the pages of this book, I hope you find yourself in the stories told herein; I hope you find your kin in these pages and feel less alone. Most of all, I hope you enjoy reading them every bit as much as I did writing them.

THE THINKER

Sometimes I sit here and think, and other times, I just sit here. This is what I've always done, what I was born to do, who I was created to be. My destiny was marked out from the beginning. I am a guardian, a watcher, a keeper of the peace, an observer, a listener, and a thinker.

An old, dilapidated, flickering streetlight - my companion and muse. She keeps me guessing.

I watch the sunset every evening – the deep oranges, the splashes of purple and pink, the dancing whirlwind descending before me in the distance behind my streetlight – and I wonder. I wonder what the following sunrise will look like, how the radiating sun peeks up over the horizon right in front of me. I should take comfort in the glorious display that greets me on sunny evenings when nature's light show gives me a final goodnight, but I long to watch the sunrise. We often covet what we can't have.

I take the things I can see – and sometimes what I can't – and I examine and wonder. I watch the traffic, mirroring the ebb and flow of the town's river, streaming on and off the island. I wonder where they are all going... what jobs have them in such a rush and irritated as they remain motionless in the evening congestion at the mouth of the bridge? I think about the bridge, about the many people who have crossed it. But tonight, and every night, I am the guardian of the gateway, the keeper of the keep. I watch the people come and go.

The evening rush-hour traffic, like the tides, has its highs and lows but endures unchanged by the Sun's solstice and phases of the Moon. I see the drivers, some having become familiar, and it's almost like I anticipate them, know their habits, and have deciphered their schedules – whether they are running late or out of their routine. I watch their faces, their reactions to build-ups, the singing, the laughing, conversations on the phone, and the most bewildering of all, the occasional tears. I listen, but I cannot hear, so I continue to watch.

My life is here, my role to stand and listen, contemplate, guard, and think. I have a lifetime, far longer than yours, to work it all out. Through such, many, many generations of pigeons and passersby and drivers in their metal boxes will come and keep me company; sometimes, I sit here and think, and other times, I just sit here.

FRANK'S DEPARTURE

It had been 9 years.

9 years of a passionately committed relationship filled with love and happiness.

9 years of us growing up from teenagers to young adults.

9 years of a union that most thought was destined for marriage, no matter what.

But, in all of life's chaos, our relationship would soon be ending as we once knew it... or so I thought.

The day I dreaded most was finally creeping up on us. We always knew that Frank would be deployed to Iraq, but we were never sure what that would mean for us. For our love. For our future. I had just always hoped that the universe would guide us toward what was meant for us.

Nine days before Frank's departure, almost as if the universe had destined it, he asked me to be his wife; a 'yes' so easy that I didn't even have to think as it flowed effortlessly from my mouth. Overlooking our favorite lake on our favorite dock, Frank said with tears filling his swimmingly blue eyes, "Before I leave, I need something that knits us together, that says, 'I'm yours, and you're mine.'"

A bittersweet prelude to Frank's lifelong dream and

imminent departure, our sheer glow emanated through the sweet, crisp air. We had "that can't-eat, can't-sleep, reach-for-the-stars, over-the-fence, World Series kind of stuff," and now, we were officially going to get to live that forever as one. Nothing could tear us apart now.

Connected like never before, I felt ready, ready to accept this challenge to preserve our love for when we will be united again for eternity.

The following day at dawn, with eight days to go, we returned to our favorite dock and intimately sealed our vows. Surrounded by nature's finest and my favorite romantic roses, our wedding day was nothing short of a perfect 'see you later.'

I am his, and he is mine. No matter what.

MY "BUBBLE SHOW"

I love New York City. More than I can say. It has given me the freedom I'd always yearned for and knew I deserved.

My parents immigrated illegally to the United States from Vietnam in their teens, so I grew up in a small, rural town in Arkansas. There wasn't much to do and not many people like me. I was different. Escaping war to find safety, my family was content living "under the radar" in Arkansas. They belonged there, but I didn't...not from the very moment I could walk and talk. My parents never knew what to do with me. I constantly pushed the boundaries, seeing what I could design, perform, and create next. I always wondered about the big, wide world, but I was taught that it was nothing special.

I was taught that being creative and chasing your dreams only led to heartbreak, failure, and disappointment. There wasn't room for dreaming when we had a life to sustain all on our own. My 7 siblings were all content working in the family agriculture business, farming and herding, but I was bored, unsatisfied, and unfulfilled.

Only a few of my family members went to school, and I was most certainly one of them. Even though school in Arkansas was still sheltered to a large extent, it was my happy place. My parents were still scared to send me to school, however, because they never trusted me to stick with the Arkansas traditions. Little did they know that they were right.

It was my senior year of high school, and as sad (and scared) as I was about finishing school, I knew that I had to make my own future. I applied to NYU, got accepted, and left on my own without anyone's knowledge or support; I packed my few possessions, woke up early one morning, and left for New York City. It was my time.

I haven't been back to Arkansas since, and I couldn't be happier. My untraditional Arkansas upbringing led me here to my destiny. I'm now getting my Ph.D. in Psychology at NYU and spend my free time at Central Park. Sometimes I paint, and other times, I sing, play the violin, or rollerblade. My favorite pastime, however, has become performing a "bubble show" right by the Washington Square Arch.

My "bubble show" is true magic, always the universal mood lifter. I can't help but intimately relate to bubbles' spontaneous nature, iridescent rainbow colors, and effortless ability to soar through the sky. I finally have a new home where I can just be myself.

THE SPIDER IN HER MIND

Zara sat alone on the subway bench, her mind racing with debilitating worry and anxiety. She had been trying to figure out what to do for hours, but no matter how hard she thought, there didn't seem to be any good options available.

She felt paralyzed, simply unable to make a choice. Any choice.

Every option seemed to have negative consequences, and she didn't know what to do. She didn't have anyone to turn to. She didn't have anywhere to go to help her figure out what to do next.

As she sat there, empty and lost in thought, she became lost in thought, envisioning a spider crawling up a wall. Typically, the mere sight of a spider would have made her anxious, but for some reason, she couldn't escape her vision.

As she watched the spider in her mind, she realized that it was weaving a web. It moved with purpose and determination, creating an intricate design that was both beautiful and functional.

Zara forgot about her problems for a moment and just saw the spider working away. She was amazed by its determination and focus, and as she continued to fantasize, she began to think about the importance of taking action, even when the outcome was uncertain.

The spider, for example, didn't know if its web would catch any prey, but it didn't let that stop it from working.

Zara took a deep breath and rejoined the present, feeling a newfound sense of determination. She knew that she couldn't control everything, but she could control how she approached her problems.

She attempted to organize her thoughts, mapping out a plan of action. It wasn't perfect, but it was a step forward. Zara took another deep breath, feeling the slightest bit more ready to face whatever challenges lay ahead.

GREYSON

It was a chilly, overcast day in the city. Grey clouds filled the grey skies. Grey cars whizzed past. Grey people rushed down the street in grey sweaters and boots. A grey shape tried to relax on the cold ground. That grey shape was none other than Mr. Greyson, the 'homeless nomad' whose name meant bad luck. He lay on the raw ground, thinking. Thinking, remembering, dreaming, and wishing.

He couldn't help but remember all the buildings – mainly the Rec Center – the supermarket, the baseball field, The Corner Store, and St. Vincent's Church. Each place brought back the vivid memories he so tried to forget... the time he and his brothers destroyed the team's equipment, the time they set the church on fire, when he had to run from the gas station because he was trying to revive his mom. Every day, city-goers walked past him and sped up, glancing back over their shoulders, but Greyson didn't often notice. He was rarely even there, back in the past, reliving the mischief forced upon him...

I've spent 46 years on this planet, and I still don't feel like I belong. Anywhere, or to anyone.

There shouldn't even be any such thing as a homeless nomad. The Earth is free. I didn't pay to come here. You didn't pay to come here. There's enough room for all of us.

Ironically, I've been surrounded by people my whole life... every day by passersby... but I'm the loneliest person you may ever meet. Some people give me the middle finger or cuss at me like a ragged pirate — once, somebody even threw their McDonald's trash at me and hit me with it. The challenges, both emotional and physical, run rampant when surviving on the streets.

My journey has never been easy, with the exact path leading me to homeless nomadism, a tragic, unfair dealing of the universe's cards. I suppose that I was destined to be here. My childhood? Tumultuous and volatile. My family? Torturous. My education? Non-existent. My belongings? Pawned.

And my life continues as such: people coming and going, valuable things left in a hurry.

<u>X3</u>

Have you ever looked at someone and wondered how on Earth you got so lucky to know them? To love them? To be in their life? I get that X3.

As I sit on the porch of our Airbnb with my husband of 14 years, watching our children play outside in the mountainous summer air, I am filled with a sense of nostalgia and longing for the moments that have passed. But as I watch them run around, laughing and playing together, jumping and reaching for the sky, I am reminded of how lucky they are to have one another- to live through life's most precious moments of such a magical childhood together.

I reflect on all the life we've been through together, from my oldest daughter Emily's first middle-of-the-night ER trip for a high fever to my middle child Tyler's first basketball game. And then there's my youngest, Claire, who loves nothing more than splashing in puddles on a rainy day.

As I watch them play and giggle, screaming like they're countries apart, I am filled with overwhelming gratitude for the joy and laughter they bring to my life. I feel fortunate that they will have each other through this crazy life and that they are creating memories that will last a lifetime.

Despite the insanely fast (and simultaneously slow) pace of life, I am reminded to slow down and appreciate the moments that we have together. It's hard to put into words how grateful I am for the chance to watch our children grow and thrive and for the beautiful opportunity to be a part of their lives.

So, as I sit on the porch with the love of my life, watching our children play without life's worries in the forefront of their minds, I soak up every moment, feeling truly lucky to witness their childhood and pure gratitude for the memories we create together.

MARVIN & MYRA

Marvin and Myra are a charming elderly couple who have been married for 54 years. Though Marvin is 78 and Myra is 76, their love is forever fresh and young – a bond of true love – despite all that had happened in their time together: a cancer scare, a house fire, a stolen car, a sick child, job loss, and wars and pandemics.

Marvin and Myra met when they were working on a newspaper route. Love at first sight almost 60 years ago. It's impossible to imagine all the little misconceptions, miscommunications, and mistakes that had to be negotiated, negated, or simply put aside. All the times they'd have to give in or give up or even keep giving when they had nothing left in their cups. And imagine doing this with the same person, year after year, until you eventually lose count.

Marvin and Myra spent their years together making memories; the couple was quite social (never out without one another) and loved playing games, dancing, and listening to live jazz. Even into their 70s, they led the church choirs and remodeled their house. They had six children together, 18 grandchildren, and nine great-grandchildren. Their joy was their love, and watching it grow everywhere they watered it.

Everyone in the neighborhood revered Marvin and Myra for their zest for life and, most importantly, each other. They never thought twice about helping people (or animals) out, seizing life's most precious opportunities, and defying the odds. It was almost impossible not to be inspired by the Knox's. Once, they even rescued a lost baby deer and worked tirelessly to reunite it with her mother in a nearby forest.

As they noticed their aging starting to affect their daily lives and interfering with their walking, traveling, and socializing, they vowed to take an adventure every day together. After all, that was their kind of love- an everlasting adventure.

Today's adventure was packing a backpack with their essentials and heading to a "Shakespeare in the Park" performance. No food or drinks are allowed for the family-friendly event, but one advantage of aging includes the right to break a few rules...according to Marvin, that is. They loved watching Shakespeare together, especially with a little picnic and afternoon wine, and no one was going to tell them otherwise!

THE NIGHT SKY

Have you ever felt alone? Cyclically and viciously in despair?

Have you ever felt so dark inside that no amount of light seems clear?

I have. I am a nobody.

I spend most of my days indoors, feeling isolated from the world and unable to connect with anyone. My only solace is the night sky, which I often gaze at from his bedroom window.

I've been feeling lost and disconnected for as long as I can remember, but tonight, the weight of my deep anguish felt especially heavy.

Unable to sleep, I decided to step outside and take a walk. The night air was cool and refreshing, and the stars shone brightly overhead. I wondered why I felt so alone in a world full of people and why I couldn't seem to find my place in it – anywhere.

I sat down on a rickety wall and pondered into the darkness, feeling small and insignificant in comparison to the vastness of the universe around me. I noticed a flicker of movement out of the corner of my eye, spotting a group of fireflies, with their soft glow illuminating the darkness around me.

For a spitting moment, I forgot about life's tragedies

and just watched the fireflies dance around me. But then they left... flew away to a better place.

I can't help but wonder if this is all there is to life. Is it just a constant struggle to survive, with some incognito meaning or purpose? I don't see any "light at the end of the tunnel" for me, and I can't imagine things ever getting better.

The night is quiet and still, but there's constant noise inside my head. Negative chatter. Harsh reminders. It's almost impossible to imagine a future where things are any different than they are now. The darkness that engulfs me is almost a burden too heavy to bear.

For now, I'll just sit here and enjoy the peacefulness of the night. Maybe tomorrow will bring new answers and new hope. Probably not, but I've got no other option.

SISTER-HOOD

Raquel, Sarah, and Delilah grew up hearing that they were each other's greatest gifts. Their mother always made it a point to tell them how lucky they were to have one another in their lives. Despite being significantly different from one another, they shared a strong bond that would carry them through life's various ups and downs.

Raquel was the oldest sister, responsible, hardworking, and pragmatic. She was a natural leader, always willing to take charge and make difficult decisions. Sarah, the middle sister, was a creative soul passionate about art and music. She always sought new experiences and dreamed up stories and innovative ideas. Delilah, the youngest sister, was the bubbly, kind, and energetic one, always eager to explore and help others along the way.

Growing up, the three sisters had a close-knit family and were encouraged to pursue their passions and dreams. They supported each other through everything, from the joys of graduating high school to the heartbreak of first loves.

As they grew older, Raquel, Sarah, and Delilah each pursued their own paths. Raquel went into business, becoming a successful CEO of her own company. Sarah traveled the world, immersing herself in different cultures and pursuing her artistic passions. And Delilah became a Kindergarten teacher, inspiring and empowering the next generation.

Despite their different paths, the sisters remained close. And when tragedy struck, when their mother was diagnosed with cancer, the sisters leaned on each other more than ever before as they faced the possibility of losing their beloved matriarch. But instead of falling apart, the sisters banded together to care for their mother, supporting her through her treatment in any way they could and never losing hope.

Their mother survived, and she said that it was because of the strength of her daughters: the unbreakable sisterhood bond that inspires others with unconditional love, devotion, and unwavering commitment to each other.

SECRET LOVER

The beach was meant for this night. For this longtime fantasy. She was out to seduce her secret lover and had every intention of making it happen.

The waves crashed against the shore, adding a romantically turbulent soundtrack to the evening. They laid out a silk blanket, and without warning, he immediately began to caress her body with his brawny hands. The air was thick with the anticipation of what was to come.

As their intense passion built, he explored every inch of her body, and when their lips finally met, something inside her stirred. She felt the intensity of their sexual union and the thrill of being so utterly consumed by each other. Shockwaves coursed throughout her body.

They decided to move closer to the waves, hand in hand. The temperature suddenly dropped, and a chill ran through her body. He whispered in her ear and asked if she wanted to take things further. She nodded eagerly, and without hesitation, he moved her towards the surf. The crisp water took her breath away as it rushed around them, and she shivered from the coldness but simultaneous pleasure.

He held her tightly against his body as they explored each other in the waves, their excitement aroused by the closeness of their embrace. The ecstasy was intense, but something suddenly felt wrong. Just then, she noticed a shadow approaching in the sand. It was another person, a man she didn't recognize right away. She turned to shield her naked body from him but realized that it was her boyfriend.

Her eyes couldn't register what she was seeing as the beach had revealed its true nature as a place of betrayal. Her heart sank as she realized what was happening. Deep down, she had wondered what would happen if she got caught... but now it was too late. She had betrayed her own heart and doomed them both to a lifetime of sadness and regret.

LUCY & DAVID

Gus was a happy-go-lucky dog who loved peanut butter, long walks in the forest, and basking in the sun. He lived in a small town with his loving owner, Lucy.

Gus and Lucy were inseparable, so when Gus escaped during a tumultuous storm one evening, Lucy was beside herself. She did everything she could to find Gus to no avail: calling neighbors, visiting nearby shelters, putting up flyers, and posting on social media. Lucy was absolutely devastated, but little did she know that Gus was just fine a few towns over.

After escaping his home and hiding in the park until the storm was over, Gus couldn't help but notice Millie and her owner, David, the next day. He saw them playing in the park where he had made his temporary home and knew he had to say hello. It was truly love at first sight for Gus and Millie. David also fell in love with Gus but was sure that he had to be lost. David and Millie stayed in the park all day, hoping that Gus's owner would eventually show up.

Hours later, no one came.

Nightfall came, but David wasn't sure if he should take Gus home with him and Millie or return to the park the next day to check on him. It seemed that Millie, however, decided for them as she would not leave the park without her new boyfriend, Gus. David saw no other choice.

He took Gus home and made a plan for the following day

to help find Gus's owner. Gus and Millie were still inseparable that night, sharing food, toys, and even smooches.

The following day, after a long night of trying to get Millie and Gus to sleep, David decided to start the morning at the park where he found Gus. He had hoped that his owner would come looking for him there. While at the park, he began calling shelters in the area and asking other parkgoers. No one knew of a missing dog named Gus.

Suddenly, David noticed a woman hanging up flyers on the other side of the street. He had a strange feeling, almost like he knew her. Lucy finished hanging up some 'LOST DOG' flyers and made her way over to the park, where she saw lots of dogs. Immediately, Gus came running, and Millie and David followed.

Just like it was love at first sight for Gus and Millie, Lucy and David followed suit. One year later Lucy, David, Gus, and Millie became an official family. Lucy and David plan to marry in an intimate forest setting with their beloved Millie and Gus.

LE TRAPEZE

There comes a time in a daughter's adolescence when her mother tells her, "Your body is a holy sanctuary, a temple."

Well, mother, I'm afraid that the temple has long been looted, and no Pope Francis will be able to undo the damage.

Living in New York for the summer, there have been plenty of opportunities I have never encountered in suburbia. Sex parties. Nude bars. Erotica shows. Swinger's clubs.

Well, sure, there are definitely some options outside the cities, but it just seems wrong to go to a swinger's club in the middle of nowhere. And I could really not imagine the crowds that would flock from suburban towns to suburban swinger's clubs.

Manhattan just seemed to yield the green light for me to put myself into wildly free situations.
It all started when an old friend, Paul, proposed to go to Le Trapeze with me. I thought, "Oh, fabulous, we're going to learn to be trapeze artists like in the circus! I can definitely use that in the bedroom."

However, if you ever tried googling 'Le Trapeze NYC,' let's just say that you will not find results relating to a kid's circus.

Paul is a complex character, one who constantly seeks entertainment. It may also be worth noting that he is a sex addict. He's the only person I know who is more sexually advanced than I am. And so, whenever he dares to jump, I must always jump higher.

As new Le Trapeze members, we are greeted by the hostess decked out in braids and a leopard-printed wardrobe. We begin the tour.

"This is the main room," she says. I see maroon and raspberry-colored velvet couches with disco balls hanging from the ceiling. I see women with half-smeared eye makeup and big nipples sitting on the lap of either a heavy-weight man, a 60-year-old man, or one blessed with both qualities. I hear myself gulp. We turn to the right to see a food buffet and a bar.

"This way, please," continues Leopard Cleopatra. We walk through a hall with closed doors on both sides.

"These are the private rooms if you and your partner decide to have some private time." I don't think Paul has ever looked this desirable. I gaze up at Paul, though, and he looks determined.

SIMPLY PUT, THAT'S HOW I GOT HERE.

THE OUTCOME

Marcus and Jamal were friends from the beginning. They grew up right next door to each other in the same apartment complex. Marcus lived with his mom and six siblings, while Jamal lived with his grandmother and cousin.

They grew up surrounded by gang violence, drugs, and poverty, with not many positive lights in their life- except each other. They saw the constant hurt and disappointment around them but were somehow determined to stay out of trouble.

They attended school like they were supposed to, but they really spent their time learning new talents. From riding tricycles to juggling and playing the drums to skateboarding, Marcus and Jamal could learn how to do anything they set their minds to.

Marcus had always been interested in the arts. He was a performer at heart and had a genuine natural talent for it. Jamal, on the other hand, was more interested in skateboarding. He loved experimenting with different stunts and tricks and dreamed of one day building an epic skate park for his neighborhood.

As they honed their talents, Marcus and Jamal found that they enjoyed their new hobbies. They spent hours practicing and perfecting their skills, and they were proud of what they had accomplished.

However, despite their hard work and consistent

dedication, they never really made it anywhere. They never got out of just practicing on their streets. Marcus struggled to find anyone interested in his performing skills, and Jamal couldn't find anyone interested in his skating talents or future dreams. They both worked low-paying jobs out of school just to make ends meet and help provide for their families, and they never had the chance to pursue their unique tal'nts.

Despite their daily discouragements, Marcus and Jamal never gave up on their skills. They continued to perform and skate in their spare time, and they found joy in their hobbies even though they never made it big. They also inspired others in their community to pursue their own passions, no matter the outcome.

Ultimately, Marcus and Jamal understood that success is not always measured by fame and fortune. They may not have made it anywhere with performing and skating (yet), but they were proud of the talents they had developed and the hard work they had put into them. After all, they started by not knowing how to do anything.

THE HOTEL BAR

Last night at the hotel bar, I was pursued by one man after another. It kind of felt like speed dating.

Subtly – or maybe not so subtly – flaunting my black blazer dress, I would allow one man after the next to get his 15 minutes of fame with me (lucky them, right?). Then, he would give up, get up, and give his seat to the next bachelor waiting in line.

There was a moment, a not-so-brief moment, in which I definitely considered just going home with all of them... together... but I quickly found myself uninterested in doing so from the lack of challenge in the matter.

Men are just so easy to sleep with. But it kills my sex drive; I need a chase. But the problem with a chase is that, I mean... come on, look at me! Any guy who doesn't take the opportunity to sleep with me is either a homosexual or ashamed of his bottle-cap package.

But, on the other hand, I also despise it when a man approaches the process of sex as if it were automatically happening. If you're going to take part in the nooky with me, for God's sake, don't half-ass it. I need excitement, and nothing arouses me more than a man who openly shows that I crazily turn him on at every turn.

Yes, I am one of those people who get turned on when looking in the mirror. So again, if you can be a challenge but at the same time act on your physical urge for me and, in effect, arouse me--- then you, my friend, are a genius whom I have yet to meet.

SONY'S PARENTS

Growing up, Sonya's parents always told her stories about their homeland, about the beauty of the sea and the warmth of the people in Ghana. But they also told her about the hardships they faced, about the poverty and the lack of opportunities.

So, when Sonya was just a young girl, her family made the difficult decision to leave Ghana and start a new life in America. They arrived with nothing but a few suitcases and a determination to succeed. Sonya's parents worked tirelessly to provide for their family, taking on any job they could find to make ends meet. They struggled with the culture shock but never lost sight of their dreams.

As Sonya grew up, she saw how hard her parents worked, how much they sacrificed for her and her siblings. She saw the challenges they faced, but she also saw the freedoms that were available to her in this new land. Sonya worked hard in school, eager to make a name for herself and her family proud; she studied long hours, sought out mentors and teachers who could guide her, and immersed herself in extracurricular activities.

And it paid off. Sonya graduated at the top of her class with a full scholarship to Columbia University. She pursued her dreams of becoming a doctor, inspired by the healthcare disparities she had seen in her own community.

Along the way, Sonya still faced many challenges. She frequently struggled with 'imposter syndrome,' feeling like she didn't belong in the elite academic circles she found herself in. She grappled with the guilt of leaving her family behind and the pressure to succeed, fully knowing that her parents had sacrificed so much for her.

But she persevered and never lost sight of the dreams that had brought her to this point.

Today, Sonya is a successful doctor, working to provide healthcare to underserved communities and giving back to the country that gave her and her family so much- a new life. She is a shining example of the American Dream, of what can be achieved through hard work, determination, and faith, acknowledging that her success is not just her own but also the result of the sacrifices and hard work of her parents, who dared to dream of a better life for their children.

ALL IN TOGETHER

We've never really had a hometown. We're a military family. My parents are Navy, so we've lived everywhere. They've been stationed all over - Japan, Israel, Arizona, Alaska, Texas, and Florida. Most of our coming-of-age years were spent in Southern Florida, which was fun. Spring break, new kids to meet, vacationers, cute boys. We grew to teenagers living on the beach.

School was fine. We joined a JROTC program - that was its focus (and saving grace). We also ran cross-country and worked 2-3 jobs since we were 14; your standard, typical cashier, grocery store clerk, pizza delivery girls... whatever we could get. As a hobby, we built model airplanes and computers and spent time in the gym... lifting weights, bench pressing, doing pull-ups, and running. We never wanted to do anything else besides be in the military.

As we got older and really thought about what our future could look like, we researched our options and learned more about the Special Forces and what the Army does on the ground. We watched a lot of military movies growing up: Silver Down, Finding Private Johnson, Flying for Hawks Nest, all of them. Our dad says that when we were little kids, we would follow him around in his old Navy jump boots with a bat and his hat and make him march around with us all day.

About 90% of our friends enlisted in the military. Between us, we joined every type of service, from the

Coast Guard and Marine Corp to the Navy and Air Force. We decided to enlist when we turned 17, four years ago. Our parents weren't even surprised when we told them. We gave them all the paperwork that was needed signed and squared away, and then off we went to basic training.

We wanted more for ourselves and our lives. That's what we got, and we couldn't be more grateful.

DION

Dion had been running ever since he could remember. Running around the house to hide from his nine siblings, running around from market to market to find those hard-to-pronounce spices that his mom always needed to make dinner. It became his escape from the world, the one thing he could always count on to take him away from his troubles.

As he entered his schooling years, he always found himself looking out the windows in class, daydreaming of sprinting and sweating on the track field outside after school. Dion came from nothing, but he knew that he had the potential to be great. He had to believe.

Even though he knew he was great, Dion also knew that a running scholarship was his only chance to make his dream a reality. He trained hard every day, pushing himself to the limits, and it all paid off when he was offered a prestigious scholarship to UCLA.

But just as he was getting ready to start his first semester, tragedy struck. Dion was in a horrific car accident and was severely injured. Not only was his running career in jeopardy, but the accident had also left him with insurmountable medical bills. Just like in school, he always found himself looking out of the hospital windows, daydreaming of sprinting and sweating on the track field outside after school again.

Dion was determined not to give up and set about

rehabilitating his injuries. He couldn't give up on his one chance to make it. After months of hard work and determination, he was able to get back on the track and start running again. Though it took (much) longer than he had hoped, Dion came back better than ever, almost like his leg somehow turned bionic.

Dion qualified for the scholarship again, and UCLA even helped cover his medical bills. After all, he always knew that he had the potential to be great.

THE EPICUREAN FLUTIST

Suki is a skilled flutist who has been performing for years. Her mother taught her to play as a young girl, and she never stopped. Suki loves nothing more than entertaining people with her music and has always been drawn to the magic of the flute. She had always dreamed of playing in a grand theater, but fate had other plans for her.

Suki was studying musicology in college when she got the phone call everyone dreads: "Your parents died in a terrible car accident. We're sorry." As an only child, she had no one else to turn to. No other family. No other supporters. Understandably, she lost her way and dropped out of college soon after her life turned upside down. She turned to playing flute on the streets to make ends meet and ultimately decided what her life would look like from now on.

One day, Suki received a call from an old friend who was now an event organizer looking for a musician to play at a "corporate" function. She was excited to have the opportunity to perform in front of a large audience and possibly get her talent recognized. When Suki arrived at the venue, her friend told her of this unique event, an erotica convention for music lovers from around the world. She learned that she would be performing for men in various lingerie sets.

At first, Suki was taken aback and quite nervous, but

she decided to embrace the challenge and put on the best performance of her life. What did she have to lose at this point? She began to play, and the room fell erotically silent as her beauty, in more ways than one, filled the air. Suki closed her eyes with no other goal than feeling the music flow through her.

Now, she is one of Vegas's top sensual flutists. She even holds private events and concerts, proudly displaying her one-of-a-kind epicurean flutist lifestyle.

AT FIRST SIGHT

I was 21 and on a self-prescribed focus on me, enjoy the present, "a one-man band." I had just ended a two-year relationship and finished a semester of full-time school. I had zero interest or time to date and put myself out there again (yet).

I decided to work full-time while only enrolled in one Psychology class during the summer, then I added a gym membership to my schedule to fill in the rest of my free time. One day while waiting outside the fitness center after my first day of class, nervous to go inside, arguing on the phone with my ex-girlfriend. A guy passed by. I peered at him, he glanced back and made eye contact with me before heading inside the building.

A small but very clear and very sure voice inside my head said: "I could marry him."

Whoa, where did that come from?!

As life had it, that guy from the street ended up in my fitness class. I fought with everything I had to not fall in love with him. I thought I was too young and too busy and that he was too Midwestern (whatever that means) and too religious. I made a lot of excuses, but my heart had already chosen him at first sight.

We had our first date that summer – we had a picnic, got ice cream, and rode bikes through Central Park. Eight years later, on a perfect summer evening, we were married there with all our family and friends.

"Life is what happens to you while you're busy making other plans." - John Lennon

I'm forever thankful that my heart knew who to love from the very first moment I met him.

THE WOMEN KINGS

We are the Bati sisters of Northern Namibia: Abena the lioness, Safara the zebra, and Imani the brown hyena. Like a lioness, Abena is energetic and strong, full of pride. Like the zebra, Safara is social, creative, and athletic. Resembling a brown hyena, Imani is witty, courageous, and intelligent.

Our tribe is renowned for its unique facial adornments and continued adherence to tradition. We grew up in competition with one another, each dedicated to becoming the tribe's matriarch from a young age. Our mother prayed and prayed, asking for help in showing our family the way.

One night, before we were born, our mother had a dream where each sister was a different animal of the Namib desert. In her dream, she saw the animals coexisting peacefully, just in the way we would have to live at home; as we got older, she told us that in order to grow and thrive, we would need to embrace our differences but also be dependent upon each other. We needed to see that each of us was special, possessing great things to offer on our own and with the others.

One morning while cooking breakfast, she cooked each daughter a different type of egg: one hard-boiled, one scrambled, and one over-easy. She told her daughters that this was like her prophetic dream, "You are like these eggs. Each is still an egg but with different textures, flavors, and purposes. Each of you has a special place in the world, in my heart, and in our tribe."

From that day forward, the Bati tribe hunted the three animals together for their livelihood and success.

KEEPING THE FAITH

Growing up in the slums of a Moroto city was never easy for James. He lived in a cramped one-bedroom apartment with his mother and two younger siblings, and every day was a struggle to survive. They often went without food and clean water, and their living conditions were unsanitary and hazardous. But through it all, James clung to his faith in God. It was all he had.

James had been raised in a devoutly religious family, and he had always believed that God would somehow provide for them and protect them. But as he grew older, he began to realize that the world was not as simple as he had thought. He saw people around him suffering and dying, children going hungry, and families torn apart by violence and poverty.

James still found the power to cling to his passionate belief in God, hoping that things would get better someday. But they never did. James watched as his mother grew sicker and weaker, unable to afford medical care or proper nutrition. He watched as his siblings struggled to get through the day-to-day, forced to work long hours in dangerous conditions just to put food on the table.

Through it all, however, he continued to pray and plead with God to help them. He begged for a miracle, for some sign of hope for them in this cruel and unfair world.

But months passed, and there was no miracle, only despair and heartbreak.

As James grew older, he began to lose his faith. What other choice did he have? He saw how religion had been used to justify violence and oppression, how the same God he had once believed in had allowed so much pain and suffering to exist in the world.

James tried to hold on to his belief, but it was too painful, too heartbreaking to continue. And so, he let it go, along with any hope for a better future.

James' life was one of constant struggle and hardship, and he could never escape the anguish and hopelessness that came with it. And as he looked back on his life, he wondered if there had ever been any meaning to it at all.

BIBI

In the small village of Morogoro, Tanzania, lived Mama Bibi. She was known throughout the village for her exceptional cooking skills. She had learned to cook from her grandmother, who had passed down traditional recipes that had been in their family for generations.

Mama Bibi lived a simple life and didn't have much money. She has always been passionate about sharing her cooking with others, regardless of whether they can afford to pay or not. She is a single mother who has raised her kids alone with the help of her community. Because they have been there for her through everything, supporting her when she needed it most, Mama Bibi lives to give back.

She wakes up early daily and heads to the local market to gather ingredients for her dishes. Sometimes she's able to barter with the vendors, trading her cooking for the ingredients she needs. With her ingredients in hand, Mama Bibi would return home and begin preparing her dishes. She spends hours every day in her outdoor "kitchen," carefully executing the recipes passed down to her. She cooked with love and passion, putting all of her energy into each dish.

When the food is ready, she packs it up and takes it to the village center to share with anyone who is hungry. She never turns anyone away and always has enough food to feed everyone who comes to her. Her cooking quickly became a staple of the community; people came from all over to enjoy her delicious meals and to connect with others over a shared love of food. And Mama Bibi is always there, smiling and welcoming everyone with open arms.

A DEEP BOND

Three cousins, Imani, Zuri, and Nia were known throughout their village for their striking beauty and kind hearts.

Imani was the eldest of the three, with long, dark hair and deep brown eyes. She had a quiet strength about her that captivated others. She was always there to lend a helping hand or a listening ear. Zuri was the middle cousin, with caramel-colored skin and bright, sparkling eyes. She had a contagious energy that lit up any room she entered. She was known for her quick wit and ability to make anyone laugh. Nia, the youngest of the three, had rich, ebony skin and a fierce determination. She was constantly pushing herself to be the best version of herself and help others along the way; she had a smile that could light up the darkest days.

Despite their differences, the three cousins shared a deep bond. Close in age, they had grown up together, playing and learning from one another. They had been taught by their families and elders to value inner beauty just as much as outer beauty. They were constantly taught that kindness, compassion, and generosity made true beauty possible.

As the years went by, the three cousins became known throughout the region for their undeniable and admirable beauty, both inside and out. They inspired others to embrace their unique beauty and value themselves for who they were, not just what they looked like. You would always see them on the move, doing whatever their community needed at any given time.

And so, Imani, Zuri, and Nia became beacons of hope and love in their community. They remained close throughout their lives, always supporting and uplifting each other as they continued to inspire those around them.

THROUGH THICK AND THIN

John and Lani had been through a lot together. When they first met, they were just starting their careers and building a life together. But when John was suddenly diagnosed with a mysterious illness, everything changed.

Lani didn't think twice about supporting John through his illness, so she took a leave from work to care for him. She was with him every step of the way, supporting him through his treatment and helping him regain his strength.

Their love was tested in ways they never imagined, especially so early on, but they never lost faith in each other. When they finally tied the knot, their vows to stick together through thick and thin took on a whole new meaning.

As they exchanged their vows, Lani and John looked into each other's eyes with a deeper understanding than most of the challenges that life brings. They promised to support each other through whatever the future held, to be each other's rock when times got tough, and to cherish the love they shared and nurtured from the beginning.

Their wedding day celebrated their undying love and commitment to each other. They knew that their journey had not been an easy one, but they were grateful to have had one another through it all. As they prepared to embark on the next chapter of their lives, Lani and John were more committed than ever to sticking together through life's chaos. They knew that they could face any challenge as long as they had each other by their side.

THE ANTIQUE SHOP

It's easy to live in despair in today's world – poverty, racism, political unrest, a pandemic - especially when you're running a small business struggling to stay afloat. For Malik, an antique shop owner, the anguish seems to be all-consuming, with each new day harder than the last.

Malik sees all too well the challenges of the world surrounding him, and it's hard for him to find any hope or joy in the day-to-day. He's convinced that his shop is doomed to fail, and he's losing faith in himself and his ability to turn things around. No one's coming in these days to buy antiques.

Malik's father opened the small antique shop hoping the community would learn to see the beauty of the simple things around them. But when he suddenly died one morning, Malik was left in charge of the shop. He never shared his father's outlook on the shop's promise and was never as dedicated to the shop as his father was.

He knew he had to do something, but he couldn't decide what that was. He really wanted to close the shop, but he didn't quite have the heart to do that yet.

Malik had the idea to focus on online sales, which could help expand the shop's reach and attract new customers. But ultimately, he knew nothing about modern technology and the modern consumer. He had another idea to reach out to the local community and find ways to collaborate with other businesses and organizations. But who would want to partner with a lousy antique shop?

Again, he found himself stuck, with no vision of how to get out.

BOOK SUMMARY

It is often said that no two people are alike; we are unique, and no one else can be 'us.' This is because the world is a complex place, filled with billions of people who each have their own experiences, thoughts, and feelings, where every individual life breeds its own journey. Some of us are born into privilege, while others face systemic barriers that make it difficult to achieve their goals. Some people find success early in life, while others struggle for years before finally finding their footing. But regardless of where we come from or what obstacles we face, we all have the power to shape our own destinies.

Planet Earth is a diverse and complicated home for humans. From the languages we speak to the cultures we come from, every aspect of our lives is shaped by our experiences and the environment we grew up in. This complexity is what makes our lives interesting and exciting, but it can also be a source of frustration and confusion. It can be challenging to navigate the intricacies of different cultures and ways of thinking, but it is also an opportunity to learn and grow as individuals.

www.ingramcontent.com/pod-product-compliance
Lightning Source LLC
Chambersburg PA
CBHW050835180626
46814CB00004B/1629